For my great-niece, Nora Jane Watson —R. W.

To my sister Shurry. You made every summer growing up special, with all the fun we would get into and the stories we would write together. You inspired me to dream and to create, and never failed to encourage me every step of the way. You have been instrumental in my achieving my dreams of being an artist and a creative, and for that I can't thank you enough.

Forever with love —B. J.

BLOOMSBURY CHILDREN'S BOOKS
Bloomsbury Publishing Inc., part of Bloomsbury Publishing Plc
1385 Broadway, New York, NY 10018

BLOOMSBURY, BLOOMSBURY CHILDREN'S BOOKS, and the Diana logo are trademarks of Bloomsbury Publishing Plc

First published in the United States of America in May 2024
by Bloomsbury Children's Books

Text copyright © 2024 by Renée Watson
Illustrations copyright © 2024 by Brittany Jackson

Bloomsbury books may be purchased for business or promotional use. For information on bulk purchases
please contact Macmillan Corporate and Premium Sales Department at specialmarkets@macmillan.com

Library of Congress Cataloging-in-Publication Data
Names: Watson, Renée, author. | Jackson, Bea, illustrator.
Title: Summer is here / Renée Watson ; illustrated by Brittany Jackson.
Description: New York : Bloomsbury Children's Books, 2024.
Summary: Follows a young girl enjoying fun and exciting activities on a perfect summer day.
Identifiers: LCCN 2023045659 (print) | LCCN 2023045660 (e-book)
ISBN 978-1-5476-0586-6 (hardcover) • ISBN 978-1-5476-0587-3 (e-pub) • ISBN 978-1-5476-0588-0 (PDF)
Subjects: CYAC: Summer—Fiction. | Play—Fiction. | African Americans—Fiction. | LCGFT: Picture books.
Classification: LCC PZ7.W32868 Su 2024 (print) | LCC PZ7.W32868 (e-book) | DDC [E]—dc23
LC record available at https://lccn.loc.gov/2023045659

Art created digitally using Photoshop,
with a variety of pastel, oil paint, and watercolor brushes to create a blend of textures
Typeset in Cronos Pro
Book design by Jeanette Levy
Printed in China by C&C Offset Printing Co., Ltd., Shenzhen, Guangdong
2 4 6 8 10 9 7 5 3 1

To find out more about our authors and books visit
www.bloomsbury.com and sign up for our newsletters.

Summer Is Here

Renée Watson

illustrated by **Bea Jackson**

BLOOMSBURY
CHILDREN'S BOOKS
NEW YORK LONDON OXFORD NEW DELHI SYDNEY

Summer is here!

She tiptoes into my room,
waking me up with her light.
Her sunrays tickle me, whispering,

Rise and shine.

No dark clouds in the sky,
it's a perfect day for play.
What joy will summer bring me today?

Summer brings me a feast of fresh fruit:
fat mangoes, bursting with juice,
deep-red strawberries that stain my hands,
blackberries, so sweet, so tangy.
I eat 'til I'm **full, full, full.**

Summer brings me and my friends to the pool.
We dive, freestyle, backstroke.

Our bright swimsuits float in the water like lily pads.

Summer brings me a dance.

Two jump ropes leap and move
and **tap,** **tap,** **tap** on the pavement.

I plunge in and with every turn of the ropes,

I show off my moves.

Summer brings me gardens, overflowing.
My family and friends gather at the park for a cookout
under trees full of leaves to shade us.

I smell summer in the charcoal on the grill that makes the food *sizzle, sizzle, sizzle,* and in the fresh-cut grass that makes my eyes water.

I feel her in the splash and burst of water balloons.
I feel the warmth of her sun on my skin.

Summer sings me a song,
serenading me from the ice-cream truck.
She brings me ice-cream cones and ice pops
and all my favorite sweet treats.

I see her in the gigantic bubbles that hang on to my wand,

then float away,

gone,

gone.

gone,

Summer brings me sunsets
that paint the sky orange and purple.

I feel her breath blowing
through my open window.

Her moon, a bright night-light
watching over me.

Her stars shimmer like spilled glitter across the sky.
I whisper a wish and say goodbye to the day.

I wish summer would stay.